Lunch With Mrs. Baskin

A Comedy
with a nice touch of romance

Sam Bobrick

A Samuel French Acting Edition

SAMUEL FRENCH

FOUNDED 1830

SAMUELFRENCH.COM
SAMUELFRENCH-LONDON.CO.UK

FOR PRODUCTION ENQUIRIES

UNITED STATES AND CANADA

Info@SamuelFrench.com

1-866-598-8449

UNITED KINGDOM AND EUROPE

Plays@SamuelFrench-London.co.uk

020-7255-4302

Each title is subject to availability from Samuel French, depending upon country of performance. Please be aware that *LUNCH WITH MRS. BASKIN* may not be licensed by Samuel French in your territory. Professional and amateur producers should contact the nearest Samuel French office or licensing partner to verify availability.

MUSIC USE NOTE

Licensees are solely responsible for obtaining formal written permission from copyright owners to use copyrighted music in the performance of this play and are strongly cautioned to do so. If no such permission is obtained by the licensee, then the licensee must use only original music that the licensee owns and controls. Licensees are solely responsible and liable for all music clearances and shall indemnify the copyright owners of the play(s) and their licensing agent, Samuel French, against any costs, expenses, losses and liabilities arising from the use of music by licensees. Please contact the appropriate music licensing authority in your territory for the rights to any incidental music.

IMPORTANT BILLING AND CREDIT REQUIREMENTS

If you have obtained performance rights to this title, please refer to your licensing agreement for important billing and credit requirements.

LUNCH WITH MRS. BASKIN was first presented as a staged reading at the playwright's home in Los Angeles, CA on January 9, 2014. The cast was as follows:

MRS. EVA BASKIN. . . . . Melinda Peterson

TERRY WINTERS . . . . Alex Weed

KIRA HASKELL. . . . . Devon Sorvari

JOHN HASKELL . . . . Philip Proctor

WENDELL SASH . . . . Kyle Heffner

THE CAST

(In Order of Appearance)

EVA BASKIN – A woman in her late sixties
TERRY WINTERS – A man in his mid-twenties
KIRA HASKELL – An attractive woman in her early twenties
JOHN HASKELL – Kira's father. In his early sixties
WENDELL SASH – The world's greatest salesman. In his mid-forties

TIME

The present

PLACE

The living room of a second floor, one bedroom apartment in an older three story apartment building in Chicago.

For my mother Minnie.
What a wonderful, wacky lady she was.

ACT I

Scene One

(TIME: Spring. The present. Noon.)

(PLACE: The living room of a one bedroom, second floor apartment in an older, traditional, well kept apartment building in Chicago. Stage right is a door to the bedroom. Upstage right center is the front door. Upstage left center is a set of windows facing another similar building across the street. Stage left is a swinging door to the kitchen. Further downstage left is a door to the guest bathroom. The apartment is decorated very modestly, yet tastefully. It is apparent that nothing has changed in the last twenty-five years. At center stage is a sofa and an arm chair at each side separated by two small tables with a small lamp on each. A coffee table sits in front of the sofa. Downstage right is a small desk with a land line phone and an appointment book. Downstage left, just below the kitchen door, is a small dining table with two chairs. The rest of the furnishings are at the production's discretion.)

(AT RISE: The room is empty. We hear the door bell. **MRS. EVA BASKIN***, a woman in her late sixties enters the living room from the kitchen. She is wiping her hands with a dishtowel. She is dressed like a woman who is expecting a friend over for lunch. She is humming a little tune as she goes to the door and opens it.* **TERRY WINTERS***, a young salesman in his mid-twenties, wearing a jacket but no tie, stands there holding his sales manual. He seems puzzled.)*

TERRY. Mrs. Baskin?

MRS. BASKIN. Yes. I'm Mrs. Baskin.

TERRY. I'm Terry Winters from the Miracle Garage Door Company.

MRS. BASKIN. Yes. Come in. Please.

(TERRY enters the apartment.)

TERRY. Mrs. Baskin, I hope there hasn't been a mistake. My company sells garage doors.

MRS. BASKIN. Yes. Yes, I know. The person I spoke to over the phone told me they would be sending you to see me.

TERRY. Well, they have and here I am, but I'm a little confused. Mrs. Baskin my company sells...

MRS. BASKIN. Yes, yes. I know. Garage doors.

TERRY. Yes, and it seems, you live in an apartment building.

MRS. BASKIN. Yes. I've lived here over twenty-five years. It's a wonderful neighborhood. When you walk down the street even teenagers say hello.

TERRY. I'm sure it's a fine neighborhood. Now back to garage doors. I walked all around this building and there is no garage. Am I correct in assuming that you have a second home in the country or somewhere, that needs one?

MRS. BASKIN. No, I'm afraid you wouldn't be. As far as places of residence, this is it.

TERRY. Oh. Then why, might I ask, would you possibly need a garage door?

MRS. BASKIN. Quite honestly, Mr. Winters, I don't. Not only does this building not have a garage, I don't have a car. I'm afraid you really have your job cut out for you.

TERRY. *(Annoyed)* That's just great. That's just wonderful.

MRS. BASKIN. I can see you're disappointed.

TERRY. Forgive my French, Mrs. Baskin, but pissed off might be a little closer to the mark. This is the third wasted lead I've had today. No garage, no car.

Why in God's name, Mrs. Baskin, did you make this appointment?

MRS. BASKIN. Well, you see, Mr. Winters, the person from your company who phoned me was so insistent and yet so very pleasant, I felt it was only fair that I give your company every opportunity to make a sale. Now, I'm especially curious about your overhead doors. I hope improvements have been made.

TERRY. Improvements? What kind of improvements?

MRS. BASKIN. Well, it seems now and then they do fall off their track and sometimes the guarantee on them is a little bit vague.

TERRY. *(Annoyed)* Mrs. Baskin, am I correct in assuming you've talked to other garage door salesmen?

MRS. BASKIN. Yes. Several of them. As a matter of fact, two of them were from your company. Of course, that was several years ago but I give your company great credit for their perseverance.

TERRY. May I sit down for a second, Mrs. Baskin? This type of customer encounter isn't covered in my sales manual.

MRS. BASKIN. Of course. Please forgive me for not suggesting that sooner. Here, sit on the sofa.

TERRY. Thank you.

*(***TERRY*** sits on the sofa, sighs, raises his arms and looks upward.)*

(Loudly)

Oh, God, why me?

MRS. BASKIN. Things are not going well for you, are they, Mr. Winters?

TERRY. No, not well at all and this meaningless appointment with you hasn't helped any.

MRS. BASKIN. I'm so sorry. Well, let's be honest. You have picked a very difficult profession. Maybe if you had something to eat, things might look a little brighter.

TERRY. At this moment, eating is the last thing on my mind. I'm very, very upset, Mrs. Baskin.

MRS. BASKIN. I know. That's why I think a nice lunch is just what the doctor ordered. Let's give it a try, shall we?

(Takes his sales manual from him)

I assume this is your sales manual?

TERRY. Yes it is.

MRS. BASKIN. Good. We'll go through it later.

TERRY. Why?

MRS. BASKIN. Well, you just admitted things are not going well for you. Experience tells me your presentation might have something to do with it. After lunch I'll listen to your sales pitch. I'm more than sure I'll be able to point out some of the areas that, when tweaked a little bit here and there, will make a marked and positive difference.

TERRY. My sales pitch is fine. The reason things aren't going well, Mrs. Baskin, is because I keep getting leads to people who have even less use for a garage door than you.

MRS. BASKIN. Now let's not be so negative. You're going to have to trust me. I've been able to help countless other sales people hone their skills and I'm almost sure I'll be able to help you as well. Keep in mind the word "almost." We all need to give ourselves an edge.

TERRY. Other sales people? Countless other sales people?

MRS. BASKIN. Probably a little more than that. Now, please take off your jacket and make yourself comfortable. I'm going to get our lunch. I hope you like cucumber and egg salad. It seems to be a favorite with everyone.

(She places his sales manual on the desk.)

TERRY. *(Sighs hopelessly)* Well, I might as well get a free lunch out of this.

MRS. BASKIN. Absolutely. Oh, since we're having lunch together, do you mind if I call you Terry?

TERRY. *(Giving up)* Sure, why not.

MRS. BASKIN. Good. My first name is Eva and it's fine if you want to address me as that, however I've found that because of my age, most people of your generation feel more comfortable calling me Mrs. Baskin. But it's entirely your choice.

(She exits to kitchen.)

TERRY. I'll stick with Mrs. Baskin. If I refer to you by your first name you might get the false impression that I'm no longer annoyed with you.

(He removes his jacket.)

Mrs. Baskin, by any chance are you some sort of serial non-buyer who dupes unsuspecting sales people into coming over on a wild good chase?

*(***MRS. BASKIN*** enters from the kitchen with a tray of finger sandwiches and some napkins.)*

MRS. BASKIN. Duped is not a word I'm comfortable with. Enticed is a much better choice. Here we are. Egg salad and cucumber sandwiches.

(Places the tray on the coffee table)

TERRY. You had them already prepared?

MRS. BASKIN. Yes. It's very seldom anyone turns down lunch. That's why I try to schedule my appointments around noon, although as an afternoon snack they are also very appreciated.

TERRY. They're very…dainty looking.

MRS. BASKIN. Yes. They're finger sandwiches. They don't get in the way of conversation as much as regular size sandwiches do. There's not the lengthy chewing. And best of all you don't need plates so no one feels obligated to help clean up afterwards.

TERRY. That's very considerate.

MRS. BASKIN. Thank you. At first I only made egg salad sandwiches but I found them to be too pasty. Then I started making cucumber sandwiches, which is quite a favorite in English tea rooms, but while they had more crunch to them, I found them lacking in substance. And then I had the fantastic idea of combining the two, egg salad with cucumbers and bingo, that was it. Do you like iced tea?

TERRY. It's okay.

MRS. BASKIN. Good. I make wonderful iced tea. It's my second specialty. Instead of sugar, I use maple syrup. It's almost like drinking a pancake. Please, begin eating. I'm sure once you get something in your tummy you won't feel so cranky.

(She exits to kitchen.)

TERRY. I am not cranky, Mrs. Baskin. I'm annoyed. While I appreciate your inviting me to lunch, what you're doing isn't very fair. Most of us sales people work on commission. Instead of being given your name, I might have gotten someone who was really interested in buying a garage door. But I have a feeling that isn't a major concern of yours.

(MRS. BASKIN enters with two glasses of iced tea.)

MRS. BASKIN. Of course it is. However, my true intent is much more altruistic.

TERRY. Is it?

(MRS. BASKIN places the iced tea down and sits.)

MRS. BASKIN. Definitely. Unfortunately, in our society, there is no one treated with more sus-pect and less re-spect than a sales person. Through the years I've discovered that being welcomed into a home by someone like me, a person who accepts them without any mistrust, but with genuine courtesy and sympathy for their discouraging future, quite often means even more to them than the possibility of a sale.

TERRY. I believe I'm about to get even more depressed than I normally am.

MRS. BASKIN. And so upon my retirement as a career counselor, a profession I dearly loved, and with my late husband's approval, this became my mission. Oh, Terry, I've seen them come and go, not just the sales people, but an extraordinary portion of door to door commerce. The encyclopedia field, the magazine field, even Avon stopped calling. And now with internet shopping, my, my, my. I see a very bleak future ahead for them and so I feel if I can offer these poor desperate souls that are still marching down this shrinking path of economics some comfort, some confidence, some encouragement and most of all some self-respect, why not? If I can meet them at my door with a smile and put a little sunshine in their life, why not? If I can bolster their self image and have them leave here with a sense that they are much more than they thought they were, why not?

TERRY. Mrs. Baskin, do you have a nice strong rope around? I'd like to hang myself.

MRS. BASKIN. Oh, please, Terry. If anything, I mean to be hopeful.

TERRY. I had hope. Before I walked in here I hoped I was going to sell you a garage door. Would I be wrong in guessing your late husband was a salesman?

MRS. BASKIN. I'm afraid you would be. Henry was a divorce lawyer, a profession held in almost the same low esteem as yours.

This is an endeavor all of my own and one I've never regretted. Through the years I have made many, many good friends who I still keep in touch with. It's a little bit sad, how many of them have had to switch to other professions.

TERRY. Did you ever feel that maybe people like you, who have no intention of buying anything from them, played a part in that?

MRS. BASKIN. No. Not at all. I'm going to be very frank. While most of them that left the business were wonderful human beings, the majority of them really didn't have their hearts in it. That's the most important part of it. Having your heart in it. Is your heart really in garage doors, Terry?

TERRY. It's a job, Mrs. Baskin and at this point in time it's my job. May I ask you a question now?

MRS. BASKIN. Of course.

TERRY. Just how many sales people do you see a month?

MRS. BASKIN. Not really that many. Maybe a dozen or two at the most.

TERRY. And these are all from unsolicited phone calls?

MRS. BASKIN. Not necessarily. I also respond to junk mail. Do you like the sandwiches?

TERRY. They're very good.

MRS. BASKIN. That's what everyone tells me. Now since we're having lunch, let's make this a little less professional and a little more social. Let's see what I think I know about you now. No ring on your finger, you're most likely single. No tie, you most likely went to college. And no visible body piercings or tattoos, you're most likely very sensible.

TERRY. *(Nodding)* So far, pretty impressive.

MRS. BASKIN. I know. Now, I'm more than sure no one starts out in life wanting to be a garage door salesman.

TERRY. Well, you got that right too. But unfortunately with no interest or aptitude in cyber technology, and more unfortunately, with just a Liberal Arts degree, and even more unfortunately, with a college loan that looks impossible to pay off, unless I marry the boss' daughter my options in today's economy are very limited. Incidentally, my boss doesn't have a daughter so that is a moot point.

MRS. BASKIN. In other words, Terry, you're feeling screwed?

TERRY. *(A bit thrown for a second by her frankness)* Yes. An unexpected, but perfect way to put it. Now let's get to you, Mrs. Baskin. It's obvious to me that you are a very lonely woman whose world now consists of luring unsuspecting salespeople like myself into having lunch with you. But there's really no need for that. Nowadays there are all kinds of programs available to older people, such as yourself, to alleviate that situation. My grandmother, back in Iowa, was picked up by a bus every morning, driven to a senior community center and brought home every evening and she would have a wonderful day. She made many friends with people her own age and the activities they had for her were amazing. Dance classes, movies, arts and crafts. When she died she had over a hundred and eighty macaroni necklaces that she made and not once did anyone ever hear her complain about being lonely.

MRS. BASKIN. Let's assume Terry, that making macaroni necklaces was your grandmother's choice. I choose not to make them. Instead, I choose to have you come over to sell me a garage door and look what an interesting conversation is evolving between the two of us. I can almost guarantee you that at the end of the day you'll more than realize the value of it.

TERRY. At the risk of hurting your feelings, Mrs. Baskin, I really doubt that.

(Phone rings.)

MRS. BASKIN. Excuse me. I'd like to take this call. I think this one-on-one we're having is really going very well.

(She cross to the desk and picks up the phone.)

Yes. Yes this is she. Am I interested in what? Adding an extra room? Well, I haven't thought about it, but I could use an extra bedroom. Well, yes, I would like very much to talk to a representative. Let me look at my appointment book.

(She thumbs through her appointment book.)

*(***TERRY*** shakes his head, rises, takes his jacket, a couple of sandwiches and unnoticed by* **MRS. BASKIN***, exits.)*

Let's see. I'm pretty well filled up this week. How about a week from this Thursday, let's say about eleven thirty? Yes, that would be wonderful. Just wonderful.

(The lights fade to black.)

Scene Two

(TIME: The next day. Noon.)

(KIRA HASKELL, a young sales woman in her early twenties is sitting on the sofa, crying. A box of tissues is on the coffee table and there are dozens of rolled up little balls of the tissue which tells us that her crying and story has been going on for some time.)

KIRA. And then…and then…and then…

(She loses it a little more, cries a little louder, then takes a tissue, blows her nose and continues…)

And then…and then…and then…

(MRS. BASKIN enters from kitchen with an open paper grocery bag and sets it down near KIRA for her to throw her used tissue in.)

MRS. BASKIN. Yes, yes. I'm listening. And then what?

KIRA. And then this morning when I confronted him he told me that it was true. He had been cheating on me.

MRS. BASKIN. Oh, my.

KIRA. *(While crying)* It was some girl he met on one of his nights out with the boys. They'd been carrying on for several months.

(KIRA's crying becomes a little more intense. She yanks the last tissue out of the box. Sobbing louder.)

You're out of tissues.

(During the scene, KIRA's crying moves to various levels, loud, soft, whimpering, sniffling, etc.)

MRS. BASKIN. Oh, don't worry. I've got twenty more boxes of them. I shop at Costco. They sell almost everything by the case.

(Rises and picks up the empty tissue box)

I have to take a cab there but I still save a fortune.

If you can fit a twenty pound jar into your refrigerator, they have the best price on mayonnaise.

KIRA. *(Sobbing)* Yes. I heard it's a wonderful place to shop.

(MRS. BASKIN exits to kitchen with the empty tissue box. KIRA continues talking and crying.)

If I didn't get our cell phones mixed up I never would have known. I was walking to my car and I was going to check the traffic and I noticed there was a missed message and when I listened to it, it was this woman and she said, "Hi sweetheart. Just checking. Are we on for tomorrow night?"

(MRS. BASKIN enters from kitchen with a new box of tissues and sets it down in front of KIRA.)

MRS. BASKIN. It could have been a wrong number.

KIRA. It wasn't. I dialed back and she picked up and said "Hi Brad, honey. God, I miss you so much."

MRS. BASKIN. And what did you say?

KIRA. I didn't say anything. I just started crying.

MRS. BASKIN. You poor thing. You deserve better.

KIRA. That's what my father said.

MRS. BASKIN. He didn't like him?

KIRA. He never met him. But he's a Republican. He doesn't like anyone. I was waiting for the right time to introduce them to each other. At least I avoided that mess.

MRS. BASKIN. What about your mother?

KIRA. She passed away when I was six. The strange thing is, the longer Brad and I were together, the more I began to feel something wasn't right with the situation. But we were living together for almost a year and I really wanted it to work. You'd think I would have been relieved to finally have an excuse to leave but instead I fell apart. Now I'm confused. Did I love him after all? And a more puzzling question is, what did I do wrong to lose him? Is there something wrong with me?

MRS. BASKIN. No. Of course not. I'm an excellent judge of character and from the instant you stepped inside this apartment I could tell you were a very warm and loving young woman. To me it sounds like this guy of yours was just a scumbag.

KIRA. That's a curious word coming from you, Mrs. Baskin.

MRS. BASKIN. I know it may be hard for young people like yourself to believe, but words like that weren't invented yesterday.

KIRA. *(Nodding)* Well, it's over.

(Takes another tissue and blows her nose again)

I'm never going to go back to that apartment ever again. I'll get someone to pick up my things and that will be the end of that.

MRS. BASKIN. I'm sure your father will be happy to have you home.

KIRA. No, that's the last place I'd go. I love my father very much but sometimes he tends to be a little too self righteous. I know all I'd hear from him is "I told you so" which is very annoying coming from a man who has been married five times since my mother died.

MRS. BASKIN. What about friends?

KIRA. I'm really not ready to face anyone I know.

I'll stay in a hotel for a few days until I find an apartment.

MRS. BASKIN. No you won't. At an awful time like this, you shouldn't be alone. Until you find someplace suitable to live you'll stay right here.

KIRA. Oh, no, I couldn't.

MRS. BASKIN. I insist. I only have one bedroom but the sofa is very, very comfortable to sleep on.

KIRA. But you don't even know me. I just walked in and started crying.

MRS. BASKIN. Yes, but you don't know me either. I think it might be fun. You'll tell me more about yourself and

I'll tell you more about myself and before you know it the pain of this dreadful situation will begin to ease.

KIRA. Do you think so?

MRS. BASKIN. I know so. Given a few days time, you'll see things more clearly and actually be relieved to be away from that...that...dip shit.

KIRA. *(Nodding in agreement)* Another interesting choice of words.

MRS. BASKIN. I call 'em as I see 'em.

(Looks at her watch)

Oh, my. It's almost noon. I think a good lunch will make everything seem much better.

KIRA. Thank you, but I don't think I could eat.

MRS. BASKIN. Well, let's find out, shall we? I have a large plate of egg salad and cucumber sandwiches that everybody finds absolutely delicious.

KIRA. Really? I've never had that combination.

MRS. BASKIN. Then you are in for a treat. Maybe you can clean off the coffee table and I'll bring out the sandwiches. Do you like iced tea?

KIRA. It's okay

MRS. BASKIN. Good. It seems to be a favorite with every one.

*(***MRS. BASKIN*** exits to kitchen. **KIRA** continues weeping.)*

(Doorbell.)

(Offstage) Can you get that, dear?

KIRA. Sure.

(Sniffling, she goes to the door, takes a deep breath to restrain her crying and opens it. It's **TERRY**.*)*

TERRY. I'm sorry. I think I have the wrong... I'm looking for Mrs. Baskin.

KIRA. Yes, this is her apartment. Please come in.

(Bursts into tears)

(**TERRY** *enters.* **KIRA** *continues to cry.*)

TERRY. Am I interrupting something?

KIRA. No. I'm just crying.

TERRY. Yes, I see that.

(**MRS. BASKIN** *enters with a tray of sandwiches.*)

MRS. BASKIN. Ahh, Terry. I thought I heard you. You're just in time for lunch.

TERRY. I'm sorry but I can't stay. I just came by to pick up my sales manual which I left here yesterday.

(**MRS. BASKIN** *puts the sandwiches down on the coffee table, goes to the door, leads* **TERRY** *in and closes the door.*)

MRS. BASKIN. Terry, this is Kira Haskell. She's here to sell me solar panels.

TERRY. Solar panels? Why on earth would you even… forget I asked.

MRS. BASKIN. Kira, this is Terry Winters. He sells garage doors.

KIRA. *(Sniffling)* Nice to meet you.

(**KIRA** *sits on the sofa and begins sobbing quietly, trying to keep it under control.*)

TERRY. Nice to meet you. Uh, my sales manual, Mrs. Baskin.

MRS. BASKIN. Yes, but first I insist you have something to eat with us. You did like my egg salad and cucumber sandwiches, didn't you?

TERRY. Yes. They were very good but…

MRS. BASKIN. No buts. I made a nice fresh batch this morning and this time I added a little basil to give it a little something special. It turned out to be a stroke of genius. Please, I insist you join us.

TERRY. Okay. But one or two at the most and then I need to get going.

MRS. BASKIN. Excellent. Why don't you sit down next to Kira.

(**TERRY** *sits down, takes a sandwich and bites into it.*)

How is it?

TERRY. Very good.

(*To* **KIRA**)

Try one.

KIRA. *(Biting into her sandwich)* Yes. Very tasty.

MRS. BASKIN. Aren't they. Now, Terry, Kira and I are going to ask you to do a very big favor for us.

KIRA. We are?

MRS. BASKIN. Yes, we are. But first let me get some iced tea for us. You liked my iced tea, didn't you Terry?

TERRY. It was okay.

MRS. BASKIN. Good. Everyone loves my iced tea. Be right back.

(*Exits to kitchen*)

KIRA. She's such a sweet, caring person, isn't she?

TERRY. *(Looking to make sure she's in the kitchen and won't hear him)* I think she's a bit of a nut job. I hope you realize there's not a chance in hell you're going to sell her any solar panels. That isn't why you're crying, is it?

KIRA. No. Not at all.

TERRY. Well, although I'm curious, I'm not going to pry.

KIRA. *(Sniffling and wiping her eyes)* No. Go head. I don't mind. It'll be good practice for me. I'm going to have to get used to telling people. Go ahead and pry.

TERRY. Well, okay. Why are you crying?

KIRA. It's because…it's because…

(*She begins to cry again.*)

TERRY. Sorry, I asked.

(**MRS. BASKIN** *enters from kitchen carrying a tray with three glasses of iced tea and napkins.*)

MRS. BASKIN. It's because she found out her boyfriend was cheating on her.

(She places the tray down.)

TERRY. Bummer. I'm sure it must be very painful.

MRS. BASKIN. It's very painful.

KIRA. I never want to see him ever again.

MRS. BASKIN. And you won't have to my dear, which brings me to the favor Kira and I are going to need from you, Terry. Now, what kind of car do you have?

TERRY. I have a twelve year old SUV that I'm gratefully surprised and relieved when it starts up every morning and if I don't get busy selling some garage doors, I'll soon be sleeping in it. Why do you ask, I'm afraid to ask?

MRS. BASKIN. Well, you see, it's like this. Kira needs to get her things from the apartment she and her ex-boyfriend were sharing and we'd like you to do that for her.

KIRA. Oh, no, Mrs. Baskin, you can't ask him for something like that.

MRS. BASKIN. Of course I can and I just did. Like I told you, I'm an excellent judge of people. I'm sure he won't refuse.

TERRY. Well, unfortunately I do refuse. I wish I could help you but...

KIRA. No, no. You don't have to explain. I would do it myself but I can't go back there anymore.

TERRY. I'm truly sorry for you but...

KIRA. It sickens me just thinking of my things still being in the same space with that...that...

MRS. BASKIN. Asshole!

TERRY. Whoa! I didn't see that one coming.

KIRA. Mrs. Baskin is exceptionally accurate with her word choices.

MRS. BASKIN. It's a gift.

KIRA. Look, if it's money you want…

TERRY. No, no, of course not. It isn't money at all.

MRS. BASKIN. Then what is it?

TERRY. Truthfully? It's my instincts. While they're not the best, I don't think I should get involved in this.

KIRA. There really isn't that much. Most everything I want is in my closet and drawers and a few things in the kitchen. It would just take me a few minutes to make a list for you. Oh, God, my life is such a mess.

(She begins to cry again.)

MRS. BASKIN. The poor thing.

TERRY. Look, I… I… Damn it, I really hate to see a woman cry.

KIRA. *(Sniffling)* Most men do.

TERRY. Okay, okay. I'll do it.

MRS. BASKIN. I knew you would.

TERRY. I hoped I wouldn't.

KIRA. *(Stops crying)* Oh, thank you, thank you, thank you.

*(Searching through her purse she pulls out a key and hands it to **TERRY**)*

Here's the key. Brad works for the city. He's a building inspector. We actually met at one of the houses that I sold a solar unit to. Anyway, he doesn't get home until after six, so you'll have plenty of time to get the things I want. I'll make a list.

(Takes out a pad and pen from her purse and starts writing)

TERRY. Wait! I can't do it this afternoon. I have several appointments. It'll have to be tonight.

KIRA. Tonight? No, It'll have to be now, in the daytime when he's at work. Besides being a despicable, lying cheater, Brad also has a bit of a problem with anger management. I'm not sure how he's going to react to this.

TERRY. Oh, great.

MRS. BASKIN. I'd go along with you to help but I'm expecting a landscape architect here this afternoon. I rarely book two appointments in one day but he only sees people after three and today was the only day we both had time in our schedules.

TERRY. A landscape architect? I don't even see a plant in here.

MRS. BASKIN. I know. A green thumb is not my strong suit.

TERRY. Well, I guess I could cancel my appointments. Chances are I wasn't going to sell anything anyway.

KIRA. Oh, would you? That's so sweet.

(Tears out page from the pad and hands it to TERRY*)*

Here's the list. I can't tell you how much I appreciate your doing this.

TERRY. Please don't. It'll only point out my lack of will-power.

*(*KIRA *puts the pen and pad back in her purse.)*

MRS. BASKIN. I'm afraid you didn't have a chance. After the first five minutes we spent together yesterday, I said to myself, "extremely uncomfortable salesman, extremely caring person," which is probably one of the reasons you're an uncomfortable salesman. But we'll deal with that later. Right now let's all dig into these sandwiches and let's chat about some of the more interesting experiences you've had in your line of work. Why don't you start, Terry.

*(*TERRY *sighs.* KIRA *and* MRS. BASKIN *are all smiles.)*

(The lights fade to black.)

Scene Three

(TIME: Later that evening.)

*(**TERRY**'s face is bruised. As he sits on a chair, **MRS. BASKIN** is dabbing his face with a first aid cream. **KIRA** looks on. **TERRY**'s jacket is draped over a chair.)*

KIRA. I am so sorry. I was sure he'd be gone all afternoon.

TERRY. He was. But you had so much stuff, I needed to get more boxes and then by the time I had most of it packed up and in my car, it was seven o'clock. Also, the fact that you lived on the third floor of a walk-up didn't help speed up matters. Owww!

MRS. BASKIN. I'm sorry. The ointment does sting a little.

TERRY. Damn it. That boyfriend of yours packs some punch.

KIRA. Ex-boyfriend, thank you. I guess I should have told you that besides having anger management issues, he's also an amateur boxer.

TERRY. Great combination. Anyway, after he hit me the first time, I tried to explain I wasn't a burglar. But then when he asked me who I was I didn't know how to answer and I stupidly said I was your cousin.

KIRA. I don't have a cousin.

TERRY. Yes. I guess he knew that too. That's when he hit me the second time.

MRS. BASKIN. Kira, dear, can you get me a small hand towel from the guest bathroom?

KIRA. Oh, sure.

(Exits to bathroom)

MRS. BASKIN. Well, why didn't you just tell him the truth. That you were a garage door salesman just doing a favor for his ex-girlfriend.

TERRY. I started to but I only got as far as, I'm a garage door salesman, because I guess he thought I was being a wise ass and he hit me a third time.

KIRA. *(Enters with hand towel)* How did you get him to stop?

TERRY. Well, remember that large frying pan you told me you wanted?

KIRA. Yes. Brad loves fried chicken and I bought it especially for that reason.

TERRY. Well, it's a good thing you did, because when he hit me the third time, I went spinning into the kitchen. Fortunately, the pan was on the stove top and when he came after me to belt me for a fourth time, I picked it up and brought it down squarely on his head.

MRS. BASKIN. Oh, my. Was he hurt very badly?

*(Takes the towel from **KIRA**'s hand and begins carefully wiping other parts of **TERRY**'s face)*

TERRY. No. Except for his tongue hanging down to his neck, he seemed fine.

KIRA. Well, I'm very grateful to you and I'm really sorry you had to go through what you did.

TERRY. I guess it's the old story. No good deed goes unpunished.

*(**MRS. BASKIN** is finished with **TERRY**'s face.)*

MRS. BASKIN. There! All done. You can open your eyes now.

TERRY. Wow, isn't this nice. I can see two of everything. I don't know what you put on my eye but I now seem to have double vision.

MRS. BASKIN. Nothing that would cause that kind of problem. It's most likely a delayed reaction to your… uh…recent, unfortunate physical encounter. I'm sure it's temporary.

KIRA. Oh, gosh, I feel so responsible for this.

TERRY. That makes two of us.

KIRA. I'm so sorry.

TERRY. Don't be. This was a good learning experience. I must never go to the rescue of a beautiful girl in distress ever again.

KIRA. Really? That is so sweet of you to say.

TERRY. It is? Why?

KIRA. You said I was beautiful.

TERRY. Oh, well, yes, you are quite attractive.

KIRA. I like beautiful better.

MRS. BASKIN. Me too.

(Gathers the towels and first aid cream and exits to guest bathroom)

TERRY. Well, sure, beautiful. I'm sure you must be aware of it.

KIRA. When you've been cheated on, you suddenly don't believe anything good about yourself. Even though I know it's much better that it's over, all afternoon I kept thinking, what did I do wrong that drove him to another woman?

TERRY. I wouldn't waste the time worrying about it. I think Mrs. Baskin had him pegged right when she called him…

*(To **MRS. BASKIN**)*

What was that word you used?

MRS. BASKIN. *(Entering from guest bathroom)* Asshole!

TERRY. I love the way she says it. She gives it such sincerity.

MRS. BASKIN. You know what? It's way past dinner time. I think we could all use something to eat. Now there's this great little Italian restaurant not far from here that delivers. And I insist dinner is on me.

TERRY. No. No. That's very kind of you but…

(With great effort stands and attempts to get his jacket but because of his double vision, keeps missing it)

…as soon as I find my jacket I'll be going.

MRS. BASKIN. Are you still seeing double?

TERRY. Unfortunately, yes.

MRS. BASKIN. Then I can't allow you to drive home.

TERRY. *(Finally getting his jacket)* Please, I'll be okay. I hope your maintenance man took the boxes out of my car.

MRS. BASKIN. Yes. Carl called when you were in the bathroom throwing up. He emptied the car a while ago, but he had to fix someone's sink. He'll bring them up as soon as he's through with that.

TERRY. Good. Well, goodbye, ladies. It's been an experience. Now, I see two doors. Which one do I go through?

MRS. BASKIN. Okay, Terry, you've obviously had a bad day, but why compound it with an auto accident?

TERRY. I'll drive very carefully. I really need to go home.

(Makes his way to front door)

KIRA. Why? Is someone there waiting for you?

TERRY. No, but quite honestly, I'd like to put this experience behind me as quickly as I can.

MRS. BASKIN. *(Leading him back into the room)* You, young man, are not going anywhere until your vision clear up. Besides, Carl still has your car keys. Now, I have a menu in the kitchen and a bottle of Chianti in the cupboard and I think we should all prepare ourselves to have a very cozy dinner. Incidentally, I'm not sure you are aware of it, but you two make a very attractive couple.

(Exits into kitchen)

KIRA. Isn't she cute? I feel so lucky to have met her, don't you?

TERRY. Lucky? I missed a whole day's work, I got my face punched in, I'm seeing double and when I left your place there was a parking ticket on my car. If there's one word I don't want to hear for the rest of the night, it's "lucky."

(He crosses to an easy chair and sits. Because of his double vision he misses the chair and falls to the floor)

KIRA. Are you okay?

(Helps him up)

TERRY. Yes, I'm okay. I saw two chairs. Wouldn't you know it, I picked the wrong one.

KIRA. *(Helps him to sit on the chair)* You're very lucky you didn't hurt yourself. Oops. I said lucky, didn't I?

*(**MRS. BASKIN** enters from kitchen with a restaurant take-out menu.)*

MRS. BASKIN. Okay, here's the menu. Now, I suggest we all get something different and share. The Chicken Marsala is out of this world and the Salmon Florentine is to die for. I was so lucky to find this place. *Very* lucky.

*(**KIRA** smiles. **TERRY** sighs in resignation.)*

TERRY. I think it's my turn to start crying.

(The lights fade to black.)

Scene Four

(TIME: The next morning.)

(The sun has just come up and the room is bright and sunny. There are about a dozen boxes against the Stage Right wall. **KIRA**, *wearing a nightgown, is asleep on the sofa.* **TERRY**, *in his clothes, is asleep on the floor with a pillow and blanket. The alarm on his cell phone goes off. He awakens. His face is still bruised. With his eyes closed, he gropes for the cell phone and shuts off the alarm. He then stretches his arms, yawns and opens his eyes.)*

TERRY. Okay.

(Counting and pointing)

One door, one table, one sofa with someone asleep on it. Great, my eyes are good. My face.

(He feels his face. Winces.)

Not so good.

*(***KIRA** *wakens.)*

KIRA. Good morning.

TERRY. I woke you up, didn't I? I'm so sorry. The good news is my vision has cleared up. I can go home now. That's a very pretty nightgown. I noticed it while I was packing your stuff. It's one of my favorites.

KIRA. Thank you.

TERRY. I liked all your lingerie. Very colorful. Not that I looked at them that closely, because it seemed a little intrusive.

KIRA. I understand.

TERRY. I tried to be as careful as I could with your things but with your bras and panties, that's kind of an intimate area and I didn't think you'd want me to spend too much time with them so I more or less stuffed them in the box. Actually, with your panties there wasn't that much to stuff.

KIRA. Yes, I know.

TERRY. They seem to be making those things skimpier and skimpier don't they? I don't know why women even bother wearing them. On the plus side, when you wash them they can't take that long to dry.

KIRA. No, they don't.

TERRY. The bras had a little more substance to them so without getting too involved, I just folded one round holder into the other round holder which seemed to be the logical thing to do.

KIRA. They're called cups.

TERRY. Oh, good name. I'll try to remember that. How did we get started on this? We need to change the subject don't we?

KIRA. We don't have to. I'm enjoying this one a lot.

TERRY. Yeah, well, I did my best. But now I need to get going. I've got a couple late morning appointments and I have to shave, shower and get into some fresh clothes.

(Gets up and folds his blanket)

What about you?

KIRA. Under the circumstances, I'm considering taking a couple of weeks off.

TERRY. That makes sense.

KIRA. *(Gets up and starts to fold the bedding)* You think so?

TERRY. Oh, sure. With what you've been through, you need recovery time. If I broke up with a guy, I would need at least two weeks. Wait, that didn't come out right, did it?

KIRA. Why don't I make us some coffee. Mrs. Baskin has it set up so I just press a button.

TERRY. Yeah. Sure, I guess.

KIRA. Good. How do you drink it?

TERRY. Just black.

KIRA. That's the way I like it too.

(**KIRA** *exits to kitchen.*)

(*Offstage*) Did you sleep okay?

TERRY. Yes. Most of the time. I need to wash up.

(*Starts to bathroom*)

You uh… You cried quite a bit last night.

(**KIRA** *enters from kitchen and finishes folding the bedding.*)

KIRA. I'm so sorry. I didn't think you were awake.

TERRY. Why? Would you not have cried if I were?

(**TERRY** *exits to guest bathroom leaving the door open.*)

KIRA. Maybe. Maybe not. Crying for a woman is not so much a weakness as most men see it, but a very important process to help us rid the negative emotions. It's, in fact, very soothing and very sensible. Maybe it's about time men stopped trying to be so darn macho about not letting their feelings show and once in a while do a little crying themselves.

TERRY. (*Coming out of the bathroom*) You don't think men cry? Get off it. We cry plenty. We just aren't that obvious about it. Believe me, I've done my share of crying.

KIRA. Really?

TERRY. Yes, really. In fact, some very heavy duty crying. I cried when my dog, Buster died. I cried when my high school basketball team, which I was on, lost the state championship by one point and I cried in Star Wars 5 when Darth Vadar told Luke he was his father… I am not an insensitive guy.

KIRA. I'm sorry if I implied you were. I just think most men seem so hell bent on hiding their emotions. You don't have to tell me if you don't want to, but have you ever been seriously involved with a girl?

TERRY. Well, yes and no. There was one. Debbie Bukowski. I was seriously involved with her but eventually it became obvious she wasn't very seriously involved with me.

KIRA. And when did you get the message.

TERRY. When I saw the announcement of her wedding in the local paper. It was then I began to realize I didn't understand women as much as I thought I did. She married our high school history teacher. I always thought she was getting better grades than she deserved. Anyway, that was several years ago back in Iowa where I'm from.

KIRA. And is she why you came to Chicago?

(Exits to kitchen)

TERRY. No. Not much was happening for me back there. I thought I'd try my luck here which so far has been less than spectacular. I've been toying with the idea of going back to college, maybe getting a Masters degree and start teaching, which is what I'd really like to do, but I'm still trying to pay off my first student loan and I'm not sure it makes sense to try to swing a second student loan. What made you decide to get into the sales game?

(KIRA enters from kitchen carrying two mugs of coffee. She hands one to TERRY and they sit on the sofa.)

KIRA. I knew I wanted to do something that would make a difference in the world, but I wasn't sure what. Then one day I happened to see an ad in the paper for a position selling solar panels and I thought well, why not give it a try?

TERRY. And you're happy doing it?

KIRA. Very. I love the fact that I'm replacing an unhealthy polluting system with something that will help save and restore the planet.

TERRY. Maybe that's my problem. I don't feel like I'm doing anything special.

KIRA. Of course you are. Homes with solar panels still need garage doors.

TERRY. Please, don't try to cheer me up. If you do, I'll have no personality at all.

KIRA. Oh, come on. I think you have a lovely personality and I think Debbie Bukowski made a huge mistake.

(The front door opens and **MRS. BASKIN**, *wearing a jogging suit, enters. She is carrying a bag containing two donuts.)*

MRS. BASKIN. Hi, you two.

KIRA. Mrs. Baskin! I thought you were still asleep. You're looking very athletic. Do you belong to a gym?

MRS. BASKIN. Heavens no. All the lifting, jumping and pumping, forget it. Why kill yourself trying to stay alive? I'm in a walking group. Every morning we walk one mile up to a donut shop, have a donut and then we walk the mile back and get rid of the calories. There can't possibly be a better exercise program than that.

KIRA. Certainly not one as sensible.

*(***MRS. BASKIN** *takes out two napkins from the bag and two jelly donuts and places them on the coffee table.)*

MRS. BASKIN. Here! I brought you each a jelly donut. Contrary to what all the health nuts say, I think jelly donuts are one of our more important food groups. A couple of these babies a day and there's absolutely no need for anti-depressants. It wouldn't surprise me any if the drug companies have been suppressing that fact for years.

TERRY. You may be on to something. Well, I'd better be off.

MRS. BASKIN. So soon? What about your jelly donut?

TERRY. I'll have to pass on it. I know if I took it with me I'd start eating it in the car and my hands will get sticky and the steering wheel will get sticky and the seats will get sticky and my door handles will get sticky and the next thing I know I've got an ant problem.

MRS. BASKIN. I understand. So then, when will I be seeing you again?

TERRY. *(Putting on his jacket)* For what reason? You obviously don't need a garage door.

MRS. BASKIN. Yes, but I do want to go over your sales pitch. I'm sure I can help you.

TERRY. Thanks, but I've been giving it some serious thought and you were right, Mrs. Baskin. My heart is just not in it. You're a lovely lady with the best of intentions and I'm glad I met you, even if you were the final nail in the coffin of my dismal sales career, but I think our relationship has come to an end.

MRS. BASKIN. You do?

TERRY. Yes. And while it has been an interesting experience it might be one that's both wiser and most likely safer to let it go at that. It was a pleasure meeting you both.

KIRA. It was a pleasure meeting you and I'm really so sorry about the incident between you and Brad. Please take care of yourself.

TERRY. Yes. And you do the same.

KIRA. Yes, I'll try.

TERRY. *(A bit awkward)* Well, I need to go.

(Goes to the door)

MRS. BASKIN. Oh, one minute.

(She gets his sales manual off the desk.)

Your sales manual. Would you like me to trash it?

TERRY. *(Takes it)* No. I think I'd like to have that pleasure myself. Take care, you two.

*(**TERRY** exits closing the door behind him. **MRS. BASKIN** and **KIRA** continue staring at the door.)*

MRS. BASKIN. I like him. I like him very much.

KIRA. Yes, he's very sweet. A bit innocent, but that could be his charm.

MRS. BASKIN. You seem interested.

KIRA. Oh, no. God, no. I'm just barely done with one guy.

MRS. BASKIN. Let me point out, there doesn't have to be a mourning period for a bad relationship.

KIRA. Well, yes, but right now it's just too soon for anything like that.

MRS. BASKIN. Maybe, but I have a strong hunch you wouldn't be too disappointed if you saw him again. And after a couple of weeks of getting to know each other better…who knows what could happen.

KIRA. Mrs. Baskin, I don't know where you're going with this, but I think he made it very clear that maintaining contact is not on his list of priorities.

MRS. BASKIN. Well, it may not be on his list but it is on mine. So I had Carl put one of your boxes back in his car. Yes, we're definitely going to see that boy again. Now, since he didn't take his jelly donut with him, I think it's a very clear sign that today I'm supposed to have two of them. Life, my dear Kira, is all about opportunity, isn't it?

(She takes a bite of the jelly donut.)

Oh, God, this is so much better than carrots. You'd better start on yours before I do.

(The lights fade to black.)

Scene Five

(TIME: Next day. Early afternoon.)

*(***MRS. BASKIN*** is having lunch at the coffee table with **JOHN HASKELL**, **KIRA**'s father, a distinguished looking man in his early sixties. He is in a shirt and tie. His suit jacket is draped over a chair. Lunch is the usual iced tea and cucumber and egg salad sandwiches.)*

JOHN. Well, when her mother died, Kira was only six and while I had plenty of help, she was still a handful. Even at that early an age she had a mind of her own. I liked that in her. I encouraged it. By the way, these sandwiches are quite good.

MRS. BASKIN. Yes, everyone seems to like them. What about my iced tea? How do you like that?

JOHN. It's okay. Tastes like a pancake. Anyway, I probably should have been more involved than I was in raising her, but the banking business is a very complicated animal. You need to be on top of it every minute of the day.

MRS. BASKIN. Yes. I've heard a bank is one of the most demanding places to work.

JOHN. Banks. There are eight of them.

MRS. BASKIN. That sounds like it would be even more demanding. And what is it you do at these eight banks?

JOHN. I own them.

MRS. BASKIN. You own them? You own eight banks?

JOHN. Yes. So far.

MRS. BASKIN. Well, I guess if you're going to own anything, eight banks seems to be as good a choice as any.

JOHN. Yes, it's proven to be a very good choice. I only wish Kira was more interested in them but she seems set on going her own way.

MRS. BASKIN. As so many children nowadays do.

JOHN. Sadly, that's so true. While Kira and I are alike in some ways, we're very different in other ways. She's one of those socially conscious liberals and I think she resents what I do with my money.

MRS. BASKIN. What do you do with your money?

JOHN. I keep it. It makes me very happy. Nonetheless, Mrs. Baskin, I really appreciate you getting in touch with me.

MRS. BASKIN. I'm delighted I could, although I was surprised to find your name in the phone book, considering your stature.

JOHN. I know. It's the one effort I make to appear like an ordinary person. Strangely enough, I get very few calls except from those annoying phone solicitors who I just hang up on. I never understood why those people keep at it. Who in their right mind would take their stupid calls?

MRS. BASKIN. I can't imagine. Anyway, John, it's not an easy time for Kira and I thought it might be nice if her father showed up to comfort her.

JOHN. Yes. Good thought. God, I always disliked that Brad.

MRS. BASKIN. Kira said you never met him.

JOHN. Sometimes you don't have to meet people to dislike them. Just knowing about them is enough. A building inspector. Come on. Where's the future in that? I knew right from the start he wasn't the guy for her.

MRS. BASKIN. And what kind of guy would you like for her?

JOHN. Well, to be specific, A go-getter, a high achiever, a guy who's got his eye on the ball.

MRS. BASKIN. Someone like you.

JOHN. Exactly. Unfortunately, nowadays, men like me are few and far between. This has become a nation of wimps, a nation of entitlements, welfare, unions, gimmie, gimmie, gimmie. Look at me. I was born with practically nothing. Did I let that stop me? No. I knew what I wanted and I was determined nothing was going to stand in my way. So what did I do? I'll tell you what I did. Something everybody who wants to make something of themselves in this world needs to do. I borrowed two hundred thousand dollars from my parents and just followed the American Dream to success. Some wise real estate investments, some insider trading, a couple of very profitable law suits and before I knew it, here I am.

MRS. BASKIN. It's a very encouraging story.

JOHN. Isn't it. And there's no reason why, in this country, it can't be everyone's story.

MRS. BASKIN. You would think so. Then again, John, not everyone wants what you want in life.

JOHN. Well, let me tell you, they're making a big mistake. Take my word for it. Having it all is everything it's cracked up to be. I fear, Mrs. Baskin, I'm a vanishing breed.

MRS. BASKIN. Yes. Well, I'm sure you'll be missed.

(Doorbell.)

Ahh, that's probably her now. I know she's going to be very happy to see you.

JOHN. I appreciate this, Mrs. Baskin. I truly do.

(MRS. BASKIN goes to the door and opens it. It's KIRA.)

KIRA. Hi. I saw a few apartments but none I really liked.

(KIRA enters the living room. JOHN goes to greet her.)

JOHN. Hi, honey.

KIRA. (Surprised) Dad!

JOHN. Come here and let me give you a big hug.

KIRA. Oh, no. Dad. You've got to leave.

JOHN. Well that sort of rains on my parade, don't you think?

MRS. BASKIN. What's wrong dear?

KIRA. He can't stay here.

JOHN. Why not?

KIRA. Because Brad is coming here.

JOHN. He is? Good.

MRS. BASKIN. I don't think so.

KIRA. Neither do I. He called me and begged me to see him if only for a few minutes. There's no way I'll ever go back to him but I'm still very angry and I thought, wouldn't it be nice to build up his hopes and then tell him to go to hell along with a few other things I've been wanting to tell him.

MRS. BASKIN. Oh, I like that idea very much.

KIRA. I thought you would. That's why I invited him up here. I hope you don't mind. I guess I just wanted someone else to see what a...a...

MRS. BASKIN. A dick.

JOHN. *(Shocked. To* KIRA*)* Did she say dick?

KIRA. Yes. Perfect word. What a dick he is.

(Explaining to her father)

Mrs. Baskin has this marvelous gift for selecting the appropriate word at the appropriate time.

JOHN. Okay, now we'll all see what a...dick he is, won't we?

KIRA. But I don't think we *all* should. This is going to be a woman's revenge and I don't think it's going to be very pleasant.

(Doorbell.)

Oh, God. That's him. I didn't think he'd be here so soon.

JOHN. Yeah. Well, before you show me what revenge is like woman style, let me show you what it's like father style.

*(*JOHN *goes to the door.* KIRA *alarmed, follows him.)*

KIRA. Dad, wait. What are you going to do?

JOHN. Stand back.

*(*JOHN *opens the door. It's* TERRY *carrying a box. He's in jeans and a sweater. He's confused seeing* JOHN *at the door.)*

TERRY. Uh, I'm looking for Kira Haskell.

JOHN. Well, unlucky you. You found her father first.

(**JOHN** *punches* **TERRY** *in the face.*)

KIRA. Oh, no!

(**TERRY** *eyes go glassy. He stands there for a moment stunned, shoves the box in* **JOHN***'s hand and sinks to the floor.*)

MRS. BASKIN. Oh, my God!

(**MRS. BASKIN** *and* **KIRA** *both rush to the fallen* **TERRY***.*)

JOHN. That will teach that bastard to screw with John Haskell's daughter.

(**KIRA** *kneels and takes* **TERRY***'s head in her hands.*)

KIRA. Damn it, Dad. Look what you've done. He's out cold.

JOHN. Yes. I must say, I can still pack an impressive punch.

MRS. BASKIN. Well, the bad news, John, is you just punched the wrong guy.

JOHN. What?

KIRA. This isn't Brad, dad.

JOHN. I punched the wrong guy?

(*He hands* **MRS. BASKIN** *the box and rushes to his jacket.*)

My cell phone! My cell phone!

(*He pulls it out and begins dialing.*)

MRS. BASKIN. Good! You're calling 911 for an ambulance?

JOHN. Hell no! I'm calling my lawyer for advice. When this guy wakes up he's going to sue my ass off.

(*He takes another sandwich.*)

By the way, I really like these sandwiches.

(**MRS. BASKIN** *and* **KIRA** *react.*)

(*Lights fade to black.*)

End of Act I

ACT II

Scene One

(TIME: Next afternoon.)

*(**TERRY**, covered with a blanket, is asleep on the sofa. A glass of water and a bottle of aspirin are on the coffee table. **KIRA** comes out of the bathroom with a damp compress and crosses to the sofa. She looks at **TERRY** for a moment, smiles and then begins to wipe his forehead. **TERRY** begins to stir.)*

TERRY. Uhh. Uhh.

*(Sees **KIRA**)*

What are you doing?

KIRA. I'm cooling your face to keep the swelling down.

TERRY. *(Sitting up)* What swelling?

(He feels his face and moans in pain.)

Oh God, my face! What made an elephant want to step on it? Where am I?

KIRA. You're back in Mrs. Baskin's apartment again.

TERRY. I am. Right. Right. Let me think. Yes, I was coming back again to…here…because…because the maintenance man left one of your boxes in my car.

KIRA. Imagine that.

TERRY. Right. It was a box with your swim suits. They were as skimpy as your panties. Really cute.

KIRA. Thank you.

TERRY. And let's see. I was actually at the door with it. I rang the bell. Some dopey looking bozo opened it. I asked for you. And that's all I remember.

KIRA. The dopey looking bozo was my dad.

TERRY. Your dad? Really?

KIRA. Yes.

TERRY. Very distinguished looking man.

KIRA. Isn't he? Unfortunately, he mistook you for my ex-boyfriend Brad.

TERRY. He did?

KIRA. Yes. That's why he punched you.

TERRY. He did?

KIRA. I'm afraid he did.

TERRY. Your dad punched me, your ex-boyfriend punched me... You hang with a very violent crowd.

KIRA. Seems that way, doesn't it. But I will say he took full responsibility. He had his doctor come right over to make sure you were all right.

TERRY. And was I?

KIRA. For the most part. He said you'd probably wake up with a headache, but a couple of aspirin should take care of everything.

(Hands him aspirin and water)

Here. The aspirin.

TERRY. Oh, thank you.

(Swallows the aspirin and drinks some water)

So your dad was here.

KIRA. Yes. Mrs. Baskin got in touch with him. She thought with what I was going through, I would feel better with family around. He being it.

TERRY. And your ex-boyfriend Brad was here.

KIRA. Yes. And that was my fault. He called me and for some stupid reason I answered. He begged me to come back, said he would never ever do what he did again.

TERRY. And you believed him?

KIRA. To be honest, at that moment I didn't know what I believed. But I knew I would be less vulnerable with Mrs. Baskin around, so I told him to come up here. I had no idea she had invited my father over.

TERRY. So when Brad showed up, did your dad punch him too?

KIRA. He tried his best to. Unfortunately, Brad ducked and countered with a right to my dad's stomach. On the positive side, it did calm my dad down considerably.

TERRY. That's nice. And you and Brad? How did that go?

KIRA. It was very strange. Neither of us said a word. We just looked at one another and I don't know what he saw in my face but I could tell by his face he knew it was all over. He just nodded his head and left and that was that.

TERRY. Well, sounds like a happy ending to me.

KIRA. I guess it was.

(*A beat*)

It's good to see you again Terry.

TERRY. Yeah, it's good to see you again too.

KIRA. Is it? When you last left here it didn't seem like it mattered if you did or you didn't.

TERRY. I guess it must have, because when I found the box of your things in my car and there was a reason to come back, frankly I was happy about it.

KIRA. Mrs. Baskin will be so delighted to hear that. She likes you very much. I like you too.

TERRY. Really?

KIRA. Yes. You're very likeable. I'm sure you're aware of that.

TERRY. I never thought about it.

KIRA. Well, you are.

TERRY. Well, thanks for the compliment.

(An awkward beat)

Well, I need to be going.

KIRA. You always need to be going. Are you uncomfortable around me?

TERRY. No. Of course not. What gave you that idea?

KIRA. Because you always need to be going.

TERRY. Yes, but that's because I…always need to be going and now I need to be going again.

(A bit woozy, he tries to get up and sinks right back down.)

But obviously not yet. Whoa! I'm woozy.

KIRA. You've been through a lot. I'm sure you'll feel a lot better once you had a little lunch.

TERRY. Oh, no I couldn't. I ate lunch right before I came here.

KIRA. Well…that was lunch yesterday. I'm talking about lunch today. You might have a little problem with this, Terry, but after my dad punched you, you were out of it for a while.

TERRY. I was?

KIRA. Yes. You were.

TERRY. How long a while?

KIRA. Almost a day a while.

TERRY. A day a while?

KIRA. Just about. The doctor said it was a combination of the punch you got yesterday and the punches you got the day before yesterday and some extreme mental exhaustion which he attributed most likely to some recent developments in your life. And so actually what is your today is really your yesterday and what you think might be your tomorrow is, in reality, your today. Does that make sense?

TERRY. Maybe if I had two more aspirin it might.

KIRA. First you need to get something in your stomach. Now, Mrs. Baskin made a fresh new batch of sandwiches.

(Exits to kitchen)

TERRY. Oh, no. I'm sorry if this sounds rude, but if I put anymore of those egg salad sandwiches in this body I'm going to have chicken feathers flying out of my butt.

*(**KIRA** enters from kitchen with a tray of sandwiches.)*

KIRA. I understand, but do your best to get at least one or two down. I know you'll feel much better.

TERRY. I'll do what I can. By the way, where is Mrs. Baskin?

KIRA. She should be back any minute. She volunteers several days a week at the local school as the milk and cookie lady. She's amazing, isn't she? To be so full of energy and involved at her age. I definitely have a new role model.

TERRY. Really? Who was your old one?

KIRA. I'm too embarrassed to tell.

TERRY. Well, now I have to know.

KIRA. Lois Lane.

TERRY. Superman's girlfriend?

KIRA. To pick out a guy who can hold you in his arms and fly you through the sky, she was on to something.

TERRY. Brad didn't do it for you?

KIRA. In all fairness to him, it is an unrealistic aspiration.

TERRY. Maybe. On the other hand, it's unrealistic aspirations that sell lottery tickets, yet someone always wins it. Boy, that was deep wasn't it?

KIRA. Yes it was. I'm not sure if that's so good for your head right now.

TERRY. Probably not.

(Takes another sandwich)

I'll have another sandwich. Seems I'm hungrier than I thought.

KIRA. How about some iced tea with it?

TERRY. This water's fine. Here's a little secret for you. I really don't care for iced tea.

KIRA. You don't? Neither do I. Mrs. Baskin seemed so proud of hers, I didn't want to say no to her.

TERRY. I felt the same way.

KIRA. *(A beat)* It's good seeing you again, Terry, but I said that already, didn't I?

TERRY. Yes. I think we both did, didn't we.

(They look at one another for a beat.)

I really should be going.

KIRA. Now that's interesting. This time you said, "I should be going" instead of, "I need to be going."

TERRY. What's the difference?

KIRA. "I Should be" doesn't sound as desperate to leave as "I need to be."

*(The front door opens and **MRS. BASKIN** enters.)*

MRS. BASKIN. Hello, you two. How is the patient?

TERRY. Until someone else decides to punch me, I'm fine.

MRS. BASKIN. Good. And you're eating. That's a good sign.

*(**TERRY** picks up his water to take a drink. **MRS. BASKIN** sees him and quickly takes the glass from him.)*

No, no. Don't drink that. Let me get you some iced tea.

*(**MRS. BASKIN** starts for the kitchen. **TERRY** and **KIRA** smile at each other.)*

So Kira, have you heard from anyone?

(Exits to the kitchen)

KIRA. If you mean, Brad. The answer is no. That's definitely over. Why I even thought he was the right guy for me is very confusing. How could I be so wrong?

MRS. BASKIN. *(Entering from the kitchen with **TERRY**'s iced tea)* Don't even give it a second thought. I've learned that if something isn't right, it eventually shows itself. You just hope what damage was done can be reversed and in your case it can.

(Hands **TERRY** *the iced tea)*

Here. I really do make delicious iced tea if I do say so myself.

TERRY. Yes. I love it.

MRS. BASKIN. Of course, it also works the other way too. Sometimes when something is right, you might need a little time for that to become evident.

KIRA. You think so?

(She sits next to **TERRY** *on the sofa.)*

MRS. BASKIN. I know so. When I first met my late husband, Henry, I really had no interest in him. I mean, he was okay, but he was nothing special. I was young, somewhat adventurous and very much into the bad boy type.

TERRY. You? Really?

MRS. BASKIN. Don't be fooled by these sweet innocent eyes. In my day, I went to hell in a hand basket several times. Anyway, Henry was everything I wasn't looking for. Quiet, sensible, a little bookish, not exactly the hot hunk all the girls were going for at that time. We didn't like each other's taste in anything, music, friends, movies… If any two people seemed not meant for each other, it was Henry and me and as far as any romantic involvement, that possibility was DOA. Dead on arrival. I have no idea why I even bothered going out with him. After five or six dates without so much as a kiss between us, he stopped calling.

KIRA. Five dates without a kiss definitely sends a message.

MRS. BASKIN. In our case it certainly did. And then one day, after not seeing him for several months, I bumped into him at a party. I was with this leather clad, super stud, wanna be rock star, who had more ink on his body than most newspapers. And there was Henry standing off in a corner by himself, still very quiet, very unassuming, probably the only guy at that party not wearing sandals and earrings. And I remember this so vividly. The rock music was blasting through the roof, the party people were all smoking and choking and yammering away, all trying to look so cool in their little world that was doomed to go out of vogue just as quickly as it came in. And then by some magical chance, Henry looked up and saw me staring at him. And he smiled. And it was a comforting smile, a warm, honest smile that said "Hey, girl, don't mess up. I'm the guy you should be with." And suddenly the room went silent. At that very moment there didn't seem to be anything or anyone in that room but Henry and me. No music, no people, nothing, but Henry and me.

KIRA. I just felt a chill.

(**TERRY** *puts his blanket over* **KIRA**'*s shoulder.*)

TERRY. Here.

KIRA. Thanks.

MRS. BASKIN. I'm sure that moment didn't last more than a few seconds. But nothing like that ever happened to me before. And I probably could have easily ignored it and to this day I don't know why I didn't, but instead I walked over to him and I said "Hello, Henry. How are you?" And he said, "Now that you said, hello, I'm fine." And then I took him by the arms, looked in his eyes and kissed him and that was it. We were married for thirty six years.

KIRA. What a sweet story…

(*To* **TERRY**)

Isn't it?

TERRY. (*Munching a sandwich*) It'd make a wonderful movie.

MRS. BASKIN. Yes, it was sweet and wonderful. And if his mother didn't have to live with us for the first ten years of our married life, it would have been even more sweet and wonderful. But it made me a firm believer that if something is meant to work out it will.

(**MRS. BASKIN** *and* **KIRA** *look at one another and nod.* **TERRY** *looks at them, somewhat confused.*)

TERRY. Yeah. Well, it's nice to think so.

KIRA. You don't?

TERRY. I'm more of a realist. I think whenever something works out it's only because someone, somewhere, screwed up.

KIRA. I don't think that's being a realist. I think that's being a cynic.

TERRY. I've been known to be guilty of that too. Anyway, I need, should and have to be going.

(*Starts to rise*)

KIRA. (*Pulling him back down*) No, wait! What about my dad's punching you? We have to talk about that.

TERRY. What's there to talk about? A father was upset about a guy cheating on his daughter. I get it. No problem.

(*Starts to rise again*)

KIRA. (*Pulling him back down*) Even so. He can't just go around punching people. He's very worried that you're going to sue and to avoid that, here's what he's offering so far. He insists on paying you the money you'll lose from missing work.

TERRY. Well, that's very generous. But since I quit my job yesterday, that amount comes to zero.

MRS. BASKIN. You really quit?

TERRY. Yes, I said I was going to and I did and since I've been in this town, nothing's made me happier.

MRS. BASKIN. Good for you. I've always felt it's as important to know what you don't want to do as it is to know what you do want to do.

TERRY. Yeah, well, right now the "don't want to do" list is much easier to come up with. Anyway, tell your dad, thanks, but no thanks.

(Starts to rise again)

And once again, I'm off.

KIRA. *(Pulling him back down)* Wait, there's more. He's also willing to make a very generous cash settlement.

TERRY. Forget it, I'm not going to take anything from your dad.

KIRA. Why not? I'm sure now more than ever you can use a little money. I'd really feel much better if you let him give you something.

TERRY. Why?

KIRA. Because he should and I want him to.

MRS. BASKIN. Maybe you should take a few days to think about it.

TERRY. Why are you so worried about me? I'm a big boy. I'll survive. Besides, I'm not going to be here in a few days. I'm going back to Iowa.

KIRA. You are? Why?

TERRY. Because maybe I'll be able to figure things out better there.

KIRA. But isn't that the exact reason you left Iowa and came to Chicago, to figure things out?

TERRY. Please stop trying to make sense. I made up my mind to go.

KIRA. I think it's a big mistake and I don't think you should.

TERRY. Now it's my turn to say why?

KIRA. Well, because…because… I guess because…

MRS. BASKIN. Because the two of you are just getting to know one another and just from observing the way you seem to get along, I think it might turn out to be the start of a very pleasant and positive…association.

KIRA. Yes. That sounds good. It could be the start of a very pleasant and positive association.

MRS. BASKIN. Developing into maybe something a little more pleasant and positive, like a pleasant and positive romantic association. How's that?

KIRA. Well, that's obviously pushing things a little, but yes, I guess that's also possible.

TERRY. Are you saying you're interested in me?

KIRA. Well, I know it seems a bit early for that, but since you've decided to leave town so abruptly, I think we need to cut to the chase.

TERRY. I obviously don't understand women. Just two days ago you were a girl crying from a broken heart.

KIRA. No, not a broken heart. A betrayal. There's a big difference.

(Rises)

Look, I'm not saying a romance is definitely going to happen between us and maybe, this could be just a rebound from a failed relationship, although I don't think it is. But I'm sure we both agree that we have become friends and sometimes friends do become more than friends and I think if that's possible it's something we'd be foolish not to pursue, unless one of us isn't that interested in carrying this friend thing any further than just being friends, which, although it's definitely not the way I feel, I would totally understand if it's the way you feel and although, yes, I would be greatly disappointed, at least I would be relieved knowing that I did everything possible I could to convince you to stay and give it a chance to see where it's going, which I feel is so worth it that I'm even willing to resort to coming off as a desperate, pathetic, brainless, babbling idiot as I am now doing because if I don't and you leave town without knowing all this, then I would feel even worse than I feel right now having to say all this. So there! How's that!

(Falls back into the sofa exhausted)

MRS. BASKIN. I couldn't have put it better myself.

TERRY. *(Rising)* Kira, from the bottom of my heart, I swear you're the most incredible woman I've ever met.

KIRA. Then you are interested?

TERRY. Of course I'm interested. I'd be crazy not to be interested. You're gorgeous, you're bright, you're everything a guy could want in a woman. I don't know how anybody in his right mind would ever let you get away. But right now I'm not in my right mind. Right now my life is up in the air. I've got nothing to offer you and I can't live with that.

KIRA. Okay. Believe it or not that's very hopeful. Now suppose a very good job happens to pop up here for you. Would that make a difference?

TERRY. Doing what?

KIRA. Well, like working for my father?

TERRY. Doing what?

KIRA. Well, he's a banker. He employs a lot of people.

TERRY. A banker?

MRS. BASKIN. He owns eight of them.

TERRY. Oh, no. Are you rich?

KIRA. Well, my dad is.

TERRY. That just makes matters worse.

KIRA. Why?

TERRY. Why? Here's why. You're doing better than me. Your dad's doing better than me. Carl, Mrs. Baskin's maintenance man is doing better than me…

KIRA. Well, so what? There's always someone who is going to do better than you.

TERRY. Someone, that's okay. Everyone, that's a different story.

KIRA. Just give it a chance. You might like the banking business.

TERRY. I hate the banking business. I'd stink at the banking business. I can't even work the damn ATM machine. Kira, I've been doing something I don't want to do since I've been in this town and I'm not getting trapped into doing it again because I won't succeed at it. I've made up my mind to go back home and trust me, in the long run you're gonna do much better than getting stuck with a guy like me.

KIRA. Okay, I see this calls for drastic measures. Since time is not on our side I'm going to try Mrs. Baskin's approach.

(Holds **TERRY** *by the arms and takes a deep breath)*

"Hello, Terry. How are you?"

(She kisses him.)

TERRY. *(Stunned)* I… I need to go. I need to go.

(He goes to the door, looks back at **KIRA**.*)*

Why the hell is it so hard to leave this place?

(Goes to her and returns the kiss)

Oh, wow. I need to go.

(He exits.)

KIRA. He left. I didn't think he'd go, but he did.

MRS. BASKIN. *(Nodding her head)* He did, didn't he. How were the kisses?

KIRA. They were…incredible. For the first time in my life I left the ground. Oh, my God, this is crazy, isn't it?

MRS. BASKIN. *(Dreamy eyed)* Yes, but so very precious and tender and for someone my age, so remarkably reminiscent of the pain of young love, so often under appreciated.

(Back to reality)

Well, you look a little drained, dear. Why don't I get you a nice refreshing glass of iced tea?

(The lights fade to black.)

Scene Two

(TIME: The next day. Late morning.)

(KIRA *is on the sofa, partially weeping softly, partially sniffling. Her father is pacing.)*

JOHN. You've been crying all morning.

KIRA. I haven't been crying. I've been weeping.

JOHN. Crying, weeping. What's the difference?

KIRA. Crying indicates pain. Weeping indicates sadness.

JOHN. I don't get it. You just met this guy a couple of days ago. You hardly know him.

KIRA. That's not so. I know him very well. We slept together. Twice as a matter of fact.

JOHN. Kira, there are some things a father doesn't need to know.

(MRS. BASKIN *enters from the kitchen with a glass of iced tea.)*

MRS. BASKIN. She means in the same room. The first time she was on sofa and he was on the floor. The second time she was on the floor and he was on the sofa.

JOHN. That sounds even worse.

(MRS. BASKIN *hands* **JOHN** *the iced tea.)*

MRS. BASKIN. Here you are. Everyone loves my iced tea.

JOHN. Thanks. So there was no hanky-panky?

KIRA. None.

JOHN. Really? There must be something wrong with him then. You're a stunning, vivacious woman. What guy in his right mind wouldn't take a shot?

KIRA. There's nothing at all wrong with him. He's just a kind and decent guy. It didn't even bother me when he fondled my panties.

JOHN. Okay, let's see you explain your way out of that one.

MRS. BASKIN. Well, when he moved her out of her apartment he obviously had to pack her undergarments.

KIRA. Normally I'd be very troubled by a guy doing something like that. But his doing it, it seemed so…so sweet, so innocent.

JOHN. So he's a nice guy. So what? That doesn't mean he's the right guy. Do you have any idea how many women think I'm the right guy. Just about every woman I've taken out in the past fifteen years.

MRS. BASKIN. You must admit owning eight banks does give them an incentive.

JOHN. Yeah, I guess it helps. Did he say when he was going back to…where is it? Wyoming?

KIRA. Iowa. No, but without a job I suspect it's sometime soon.

JOHN. So he's still in town.

KIRA. I guess so.

JOHN. Okay, we need to come up with a plan to keep him in town until we work out a plan to make him want to stay in town. Now are you sure he can't be bought?

MRS. BASKIN. Not a chance.

JOHN. I hate those kind of people.

KIRA. This is very degrading. The last thing I want is for you to buy me a boyfriend.

JOHN. Well, what if I didn't try to buy him? What if I just tried to rent him for a while?

KIRA. Please, dad. This is very difficult for me.

JOHN. Yes. And I am having great difficulty trying to figure something out so it won't be so difficult. Look, what if I sat down with him face to face and said, listen kid…

KIRA. And?

JOHN. That's all I've got so far.

KIRA. What's the use. Chances are we'll never see each other again.

MRS. BASKIN. Well, not necessarily. As a matter of fact, I'm expecting him here very shortly.

KIRA. You are?

MRS. BASKIN. Yes. It seems there was another box of your things in his car.

KIRA. Again?

MRS. BASKIN. I wasn't sure how things were going to work out yesterday, so I had Carl put it in just in case. On my walk this morning I called Terry and asked him to drop it off this afternoon. There's no doubt in my mind, Kira, that he has the same strong feelings for you that you have for him. He just needs to be convinced not to run away from them.

JOHN. How do we accomplish that?

MRS. BASKIN. That is going to take some special doing.

(Doorbell.)

KIRA. Oh, no. He's here.

JOHN. Okay, I'll be careful not to scare him away. I'm going to try to smile.

(Wide smile)

What do you think of this?

MRS. BASKIN. Maybe smiling isn't for you, John.

*(**MRS. BASKIN** opens the door. **WENDELL SASH**, A man in his mid-forties stands there.)*

WENDELL. Mrs. Baskin. How are you?

(Kisses her on the cheek)

MRS. BASKIN. Wendell it's so good to see you again. Come in.

(She brings him into the living room.)

I'd like you both to meet my good friend, Wendell Sash. Wendell is a salesman for the Decorative Driveway Company. Wendell, this is John Haskell and his lovely daughter Kira that I spoke to you about.

WENDELL. *(Taking **KIRA**'s hand)* Lovely is much too mild a word.

(Shaking **JOHN***'s hand)*

However, looking at you John I can see where she gets that regal quality from.

JOHN. *(Impressed)* You're good.

MRS. BASKIN. Isn't he?

JOHN. Decorative driveways, huh?

WENDELL. Yes, you know, cobblestone, slate, limestone, sandstone… Driveways that give your home that special look that ordinary, dull asphalt and cement can't.

MRS. BASKIN. Wendell was planning to be in the neighborhood today so I asked him to stop by. Wendell is probably the best salesman I've had the pleasure of meeting and as you know by now, I've met many.

JOHN. *(Skeptical)* The best salesman Mrs. Baskin ever met. I'm sure Mrs. Baskin doesn't toss that accolade around frivolously. I'm curious. What is it you do that won you that special honor?

WENDELL. It's all in the approach. First of all it's very important to know the nature of the potential buyer. There are basically two types. Those that want your product and those that don't.

JOHN. Well, let's say you come up against a guy like me. I can guarantee you I don't and I won't.

*(***WENDELL*** puts his arm around ***JOHN****'s shoulder and during the following walks him around the room.)*

WENDELL. Not a problem, John. Fundamentally, what I use is a three step process, although I very seldom need to use the third step. In the first step I appeal to your sense of the esthetic. I point out how much warmer and inviting a decorative driveway would make your home look. Just out of curiosity, what sort of house do you live in John?

JOHN. I live in a very fine, solid, two story red brick house with a very fine, very solid concrete circular driveway that I'm perfectly satisfied with.

WENDELL. Right and you'll most likely remain perfectly satisfied with it as long as you don't think about something else.

JOHN. Like what, I'm going to foolishly ask?

WENDELL. Like an awesome, elegant, matching red brick, circular driveway. An awesome, elegant, matching red brick, circular driveway that would turn that very fine, solid, two story red brick house of yours into a much more eye catching and breathtaking structure than it already is.

JOHN. Okay, easy enough. I won't think about an awesome, elegant, matching red brick, circular driveway. Now what?

WENDELL. Now I go to step two and produce documentation proving that if you did put in this awesome, elegant, matching red brick, circular driveway, almost immediately the value of your very fine, solid, two story red brick house increases by twice what that awesome, elegant, matching red brick, circular driveway cost. And then with inflation being what it is, well, figure it out John. By not putting in this awesome, elegant, matching red brick, circular driveway, you will actually be losing money.

JOHN. A good point to make, unless of course you're as astute as I am at wheeling and dealing with fluctuating interest rates, which for me has proven to be a stupendous area of profit and a much better use of my financial resources than for an awesome, elegant, matching red brick, circular driveway. So while your second step was a good effort, it's still not good enough for a person of my ilk. So far, Mrs. Baskin, I'm not impressed.

MRS. BASKIN. It's obvious you're a step three kind of guy John. Finish him off, Wendell.

WENDELL. Right. Well, John, in this third and final step I appeal to your great pride in being who you are. Your ego, your vanity and the rapture of being you. I point

out the fact that every time you look out your front
window at that awesome, elegant, matching red brick,
circular driveway, that incredibly stunning, impressive,
awesome, elegant, matching red brick, circular
driveway that both you and I know, you don't really
want.

JOHN. No, I don't.

WENDELL. You don't really need.

JOHN. No, I don't.

WENDELL. That majestic, outrageously over-priced, self-
indulgent, elegant, awesome, matching red brick,
circular driveway, that frankly, only a very select
few can afford, will be saying, not just to you, to
your neighbors, to your business associates, to your
mailman, to your gardener, to your friends as well as
your enemies, to every living man, woman and child
who sees it, drives by it, walks by it…

JOHN. What? What? What will it be saying?

WENDELL. It will be saying "Hey, look at me America. My
name is John Haskell and like it or not, I've got the
world by the balls!"

(There is a moment of awesome silence.)

JOHN. How soon can you start working on it?

WENDELL. I'll have a crew at your house first thing in the
morning.

JOHN. Let's do it.

KIRA. *(Stunned)* Oh, my gosh. I can't believe what I saw.

MRS. BASKIN. He's remarkable isn't he?

JOHN. *(Dazed. He sits.)* It's insane. I'm buying a driveway I
don't even need or want. The son-of-a bitch is good.

(Doorbell.)

MRS. BASKIN. That's probably Terry. I'll get it.

*(She opens the door. It's **TERRY** with a box.)*

Terry. Come in.

TERRY. I really can't stay very long.

MRS. BASKIN. Oh, stop it and come in.

(She pulls TERRY *in and closes the door.* TERRY *puts the box down and follows her to* KIRA, JOHN *and* WENDELL.*)*

KIRA. Hi.

TERRY. Hi. A box of your things were in my car. What a surprise, huh?

MRS. BASKIN. Yes, well, we'll deal with all that later. First let me introduce everyone. Terry Winters, I want you to meet my dear friend Wendell Sash. Wendell is a driveway salesman.

TERRY. Isn't he lucky.

WENDELL. Very lucky as a matter of fact. I just sold another driveway about a minute ago.

TERRY. To who?

JOHN. To me. And it was the last thing I thought I wanted.

(Stands up)

MRS. BASKIN. And of course Terry, you sort of met Kira's father, John Haskell.

JOHN. Nice to see you again, young man.

TERRY. *(Nodding)* Mr. Haskell.

JOHN. Please, call me John. I can't begin to tell you how sorry I am for the mix-up and I'm more than ready and willing to rectify my inappropriate behavior however I can.

TERRY. Thanks, but I already told your daughter, there's no need to pursue that incident any further. It's all forgotten.

JOHN. Yes, I know and I think you're making a big mistake because you are in a wonderful position to take great advantage of me. A situation like this does not come along that often.

TERRY. Good. Because I don't think my face can take another punch.

MRS. BASKIN. Incidentally, Wendell, Terry is a garage door salesman.

TERRY. <u>Was</u> a garage door salesman. I'm between depressing careers.

WENDELL. Really? Well who hasn't been there?

JOHN. I haven't.

MRS. BASKIN. Unfortunately, that's not the only difficulty Terry seems to be facing. He has one much bigger than that.

TERRY. I do?

MRS. BASKIN. Of course you do and you know very well what I'm talking about. I have spent several days with these two young people and if any two people should be together, it's them.

WENDELL. How nice. So what's the problem?

MRS. BASKIN. The problem is he is on the verge of making the biggest mistake of his life by running away from it.

WENDELL. Really?

TERRY. Mrs. Baskin, this is a little uncomfortable.

MRS. BASKIN. Yes, I know. But this is the obstacle we're facing and we need to find a way to remedy it.

TERRY. Now look, before everyone jumps to conclusions, I think any guy who ends up with Kira has to consider himself the luckiest guy in the world and there's nothing more I could ever wish for than being that guy.

JOHN. So what's the problem?

TERRY. The problem is that I'm at a point in my life where I need to prove to myself I'm not a loser and it's possible I may never do it.

KIRA. I don't believe that for a minute.

TERRY. Then believe this. The last thing I want is watching you watching me fail my way through life. You don't need that. You don't deserve that.

JOHN. Well, what if I gave you a bank? Would that make a difference?

MRS. BASKIN. Oh, that's a good idea.

TERRY. That's not what this is about.

KIRA. First of all, Terry, you're not a loser. I know losers. You're just very proud. And that's fine. But there's a point where pride can lead to irrational decisions.

JOHN. What if I gave you two banks?

KIRA. Dad, please.

TERRY. Look, you've already had one bad experience with a guy you thought you knew. Why risk having another bad experience with someone you know even less?

KIRA. I know you better than you do and your doubts and fears are totally unfounded.

WENDELL. Can I say something?

MRS. BASKIN. Of course.

WENDELL. Everyone sit down because this is going to take a while.

JOHN. *(Sarcastic)* Good. Maybe it'll give me time to rethink my new driveway.

(Everyone but **WENDELL** *sits.)*

WENDELL. This is all so…so surreal. I am seeing my story.

KIRA. You are?

WENDELL. I am. When I met my wife, Rebecca, I had nothing. I had no idea where I was going, and like you, Terry, I was frightened to death I was going nowhere. I had more fear than I ever had before. Fear that I wouldn't be able to provide her with the decent home she deserved. Fear that I wouldn't be able to support the family I knew we wanted. Fear that she would soon see what a bad choice she made and I would eventually lose her. But the thought of not being with her, of going through life without her, of not waking up every morning and finding her by my side, this absolutely fantastic woman who I loved more than I ever thought I could love anyone… It was too painful to even imagine. And so against my better judgment, against all common sense, I took the plunge. We got married.

JOHN. Good for you. I did the same thing six times.

WENDELL. Yes, it was good for me. And do you know why?

JOHN. No, why?

MRS. BASKIN. Yes, please tell us, Wendell.

WENDELL. My being with her was the turning point. My commitment to her, to this wonderful woman, was the one piece of my life that had been missing. I needed that commitment because with it I became even more determined not to fail.

JOHN. This is powerful stuff! I like it!

MRS. BASKIN. Good. Go on Wendell.

WENDELL. Sure, until I found my niche, I did have a few rocky bumps. But with someone who loved me as unconditionally as Rebecca did, with someone to encourage me as my beautiful Rebecca did, to hold my hand when things didn't go well… To comfort me. To strengthen me. To calm my fears. To always be there with her smile, her kisses, her touch. With someone as wonderful as my darling Rebecca to hold in my arms every night, I refused to quit, I refused to say, "poor me," and so every day I went out there determined to kick ass and by God, I did.

JOHN. Now that's my kind of man.

(Applauds)

Bravo! Bravo!

MRS. BASKIN. It's a fascinating story, Wendell. Absolutely fascinating and uplifting.

WENDELL. Thank you. Today we have two children in college. Frances is in her third year of medical school and Albert, well on his way to becoming a Constitutional lawyer. Two fine young, dedicated citizens who are determined to make this world a better place.

And because I chose love over pride, because I chose love over doubt in myself, I've had a life with a woman I love today every bit as much as I did twenty five years ago when I married her. A woman who, without her in my corner, I know I could never have ended up as successful, as unbelievably happy as I am now.

JOHN. That's just beautiful. Look!

(Points to his eyes)

My eyes are actually watering up. Can you believe it? Real tears.

*(**MRS. BASKIN** hands **JOHN** a tissue.)*

MRS. BASKIN. Have a tissue, John.

JOHN. Thank you.

(He blows his nose into it.)

(They all react.)

Sorry.

(Stuffs the tissue in his pocket)

Continue, Wendell.

WENDELL. *(Continuing)* Listen to me, Terry. Don't let this moment escape you. My story can be your story. Don't be afraid to take the chance that I did. It's the greatest gift you can give to yourself. It's the greatest gift you can give to your future, to the woman you love, to the children you're destined to have. With her at your side, you are complete. To let her get away would be the most foolish thing you could ever do.

JOHN. *(To **TERRY**)* What if I gave you two banks and some beach front property in Florida?

KIRA. Dad!

TERRY. *(Getting up)* Okay, okay. That was good. That was very good. Not your dad's offer, but Wendell's story. I liked it as much as I liked Mrs. Baskin's story that she told us yesterday. It was hopeful, it was positive and okay, the truth is I really don't want to walk away from this and if there's a chance in a million that Wendell's story can be Kira's and my story, then I need to take it.

JOHN. That's my boy…hopefully.

TERRY. But before I go on, I need to do this right now or I'll go crazy.

(He goes to **KIRA**, *pulls her to her feet.)*

Hello, Kira. How are you?

(He kisses her.)

MRS. BASKIN. Oh, John. Isn't that beautiful?

JOHN. Yes. And except for the damn driveway it hasn't cost me anything.

TERRY. You're right! You're all right! The last thing I want to do is lose this wonderful…wonderful person.

(To **KIRA***)*

Okay, Kira. If you really want to take a chance with me, let's do it. I assume it's okay with you, John.

JOHN. She's happy. I'm happy.

KIRA. I'm very happy.

TERRY. Great. Then this is what I'm going to do to make it work. I'm going back to school to get my Master's degree so I can teach.

MRS. BASKIN. Good for you. A most noble profession.

JOHN. *(Outraged)* What? I raised my daughter to be the wife of a teacher? Never! For God's sake, Kira. Why would you want to live below the poverty line?

KIRA. Please, Dad.

TERRY. No, he's right. So, I'll up that. I'll go back for a PhD and become a Professor. How's that?

JOHN. A little better. Get a few years under your belt and I'll buy you your own college.

TERRY. Let's put that thought on hold. But here's how you can help now. In order to go back to school I'll need a second student loan to pay off my first student loan so I can get a third student loan. You're a banker, John. How about it?

JOHN. A student loan? Those are a little tricky and I'm sorry to say not a good risk for a bank to take. What if

I just gave you the money then there's no red ink on the books?

TERRY. No. I'm not taking any money from you. Wendell convinced me. Kira and I need to make this struggle together. It has to be a loan.

JOHN. Okay, Okay. How's fifty thousand dollars at twelve percent? I'm pretty sure I can swing that.

TERRY. Sounds lousy, but I'm not very good at negotiating.

MRS. BASKIN. I've gotten to know John fairly well. Let me take it from here. School is not cheap, John. I'm thinking one hundred thousand at three percent.

JOHN. Try thinking sixty thousand at ten percent.

MRS. BASKIN. Ninety thousand at four.

JOHN. Seventy thousand at eight.

MRS. BASKIN. Screw you, John. We're going to another bank.

JOHN. All right! All right! Ninety thousand at four. I'll cut a check first thing in the morning. Damn it, I'm losing my touch.

KIRA. *(To* **TERRY***)* Well, now what?

TERRY. Now you and I are going to find a little coffee shop, sit down by ourselves, take a couple of deep breaths and without any pressures or manipulations, try to figure out what we do next.

KIRA. I have a few ideas but they don't involve a coffee shop.

TERRY. We'll get to those later. Nice meeting you Wendell. Let's stay in touch. And John…

JOHN. *(Hopeful)* Yes?

TERRY. I'm sure you'll grow on me.

(Takes **KIRA***'s hand)*

C'mon, Kira.

(Leads her to the door)

KIRA. Bye everyone.

*(**TERRY** opens the door and then turns to the group.)*

TERRY. You know, Mrs. Baskin, when I first met you I thought you were just a lonely wacky lady. Then as I got to know you, I thought you were just a sweet wacky lady. I haven't changed my mind about the wacky part but I'd like to insert a new adjective. Incredible. See you.

*(He and **KIRA** exit.)*

WENDELL. That's the first time I've heard anyone use the word "adjective" since I've been out of grade school. He's obviously very bright.

MRS. BASKIN. Well, I'm going to use another adjective. Perfect! Because that's the way this all worked out.

JOHN. Yes, it did. And I can't thank both of you enough. I need to tell you Wendell, how much I was moved by your heartfelt story of you and your wife and those wonderful children you brought into this world. It was one of the most touching and encouraging moments I've ever experienced.

WENDELL. Well, thank you so much, John. Too bad it wasn't true.

JOHN. Excuse me?

WENDELL. Not a word of it was true.

MRS. BASKIN. I'm afraid Wendell has almost as bad a marital track record as you John.

JOHN. He does?

WENDELL. Unfortunately John, you're looking at a three time loser. They all complained about the same thing. That I loved being a salesman more than I loved being a husband. As good a salesman as I am, I couldn't convince them they were wrong.

JOHN. *(Disbelief)* It wasn't true. You and Rebecca and Frances and Albert, it was all bullshit?

MRS. BASKIN. I told you he was the best salesman I ever met.

WENDELL. You see, John, when Mrs. Baskin called me last night and told me what the problem was between those two kids, we decided this was the best way to solve it.

JOHN. Is that so, Mrs. Baskin. You arranged this?

MRS. BASKIN. While I truly do believe that if something is meant to work out it will, now and then you have to give it a little nudge.

WENDELL. I hope you're not angry, John.

JOHN. Angry. I am so impressed I can't put it into words. To be so deceiving, so misleading with such a straight, convincing face... Wendell, how would you like to go into the banking business?

WENDELL. It's something we can discuss over lunch. I don't think I need to tell you, Mrs. Baskin, I've been looking forward to those cute little egg salad and cucumber sandwiches all morning long.

MRS. BASKIN. I'm so happy to hear that. I actually made a double batch today. I'll bring them right out. Yes, this day has turned out quite superbly, hasn't it?

JOHN. Yes. Yes it has.

(*As she starts towards the kitchen, the phone rings.*)

MRS. BASKIN. Let me get that first.

WENDELL. Of course.

(*She picks up the phone.*)

MRS. BASKIN. Yes. Yes this is she. What? Weather proof aluminum siding? Wait, I'll see.

(*To the two men*)

Am I interested in talking to someone about weather proof aluminum siding?

JOHN AND WENDELL. Absolutely!

MRS. BASKIN. (*On phone*) Absolutely!

(*The lights begin to dim on the two men. A spot begins to tighten on* **MRS. BASKIN**.)

(Opening her appointment book)

Let's see. How about if we booked an appointment for sometime next week, shall we say about noon?

(The lights fade to black.)

The End

PROPS

ACT I

Scene 1
  Dish towel
  Garage Door Sales Manual
  Tray of egg salad and cucumber finger sandwiches
  Napkins
  2 glasses of iced tea

Scene 2
  Box of tissues
  A dozen crumpled tissues
  Paper grocery bag
  Tray of egg salad and cucumber finger sandwiches
  Tray with 3 glasses of iced tea
  Napkins
  KIRA's handbag
  Paper, pen and key (in **KIRA**'s handbag)

Scene 3
  Tube of first aid cream and cotton balls
  Hand towel
  Restaurant take-out menu

Scene 4
  Several medium size packing boxes
  Pillow and blanket for sofa
  Pillow and blanket for floor
  TERRY's cell phone
  2 mugs of coffee
  2 jelly donuts and napkins in a bag
  Garage Door Sales Manual

Scene 5
  Tray of egg salad and cucumber finger sandwiches
  2 glasses of iced tea
  JOHN's cell phone
  Medium size packing box

PROPS – CONTINUED

ACT II

Scene 1

    Pillow and blanket for sofa
    Glass of water
    Bottle of aspirin
    Damp compress
    Tray of egg salad and cucumber finger sandwiches
    Glass of iced tea

Scene 2

    Glass of iced tea
    Medium size packing box
    Box of tissue

COSTUMES

ACT I

Scene 1

MRS. BASKIN – A pleasant dress
TERRY – Pants, jacket, shirt

Scene 2

KIRA – Jacket, skirt, blouse
MRS. BASKIN – Another pleasant dress
TERRY – Pants, different jacket and shirt

Scene 3

Same as Scene 2

Scene 4

TERRY – Same as Scene 2
KIRA – Night gown
MRS. BASKIN – Jogging suit

Scene 5

JOHN – Conservative business suit, shirt and tie
MRS. BASKIN – Another pleasant dress
KIRA – Casual slacks suit
TERRY – Jeans, sweater, sneakers

ACT II

Scene 1

TERRY – Same as Act I, Scene 5
KIRA – Blouse and skirt
MRS. BASKIN – Another pleasant dress

Scene 2

JOHN – Another conservative business suit, shirt and tie
KIRA – Slacks and sweater
MRS. BASKIN – Another pleasant dress
WENDELL – Jacket, pants, turtleneck
TERRY – Jeans and a different sweater

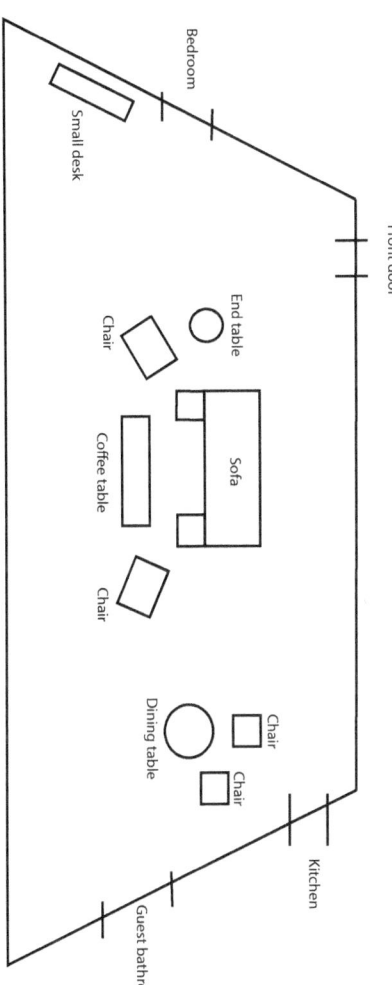

Lunch with Mrs. Baskin Set Design